This edition first published in 2014 by Gecko Press
PO Box 9335, Marion Square, Wellington 6141, New Zealand
info@geckopress.com

This edition © Gecko Press Ltd 2014

Distributed in the United Kingdom by Bounce Sales and Marketing,
www.bouncemarketing.co.uk
Distributed in Australia by Scholastic Australia,
www.scholastic.com.au
Distributed in New Zealand by Random House NZ,
www.randomhouse.co.nz

A catalogue record for this book is available from the
National Library of New Zealand.

Original title: L'ami paresseux
Story and illustrations: Ronan Badel
Copyright © 2014, éditions Autrement
Translation copyright © 2014, Gecko Press

Design by Spencer Levine, New Zealand
Printed in China by Everbest Printing Co Ltd,
an accredited ISO 14001 & FSC certified printer

Hardback ISBN: 978-1-927271-41-4

For more curiously good books, visit www.geckopress.com

the lazy friend

ronan badel

GECKO PRESS